FUNNY ANIMALS

4 Easy-to-Read Stories

More Spaghetti, I Say!
The Day the Dog Said, "Cock-a-Doodle-Doo!"
Two Crazy Pigs
Fraidy Cats

SCHOLASTIC INC. Cartwheel B·O·O·K·S®

New York Toronto London Auckland Sydney
Mexico City New Delhi Hong Kong Buenos Aires

More Spaghetti, I Say! (0-590-45783-7)
Text copyright © 1993 by Rita Golden Gelman.
Illustrations copyright © 1993 by Mort Gerberg.

The Day the Dog Said, "Cock-a-Doodle-Doo!" (0-590-73887-9)
Copyright © 1997 by David McPhail.

Two Crazy Pigs (0-590-44972-9)
Text copyright © 1992 by Karen Nagel.
Illustrations copyright © 1992 by Brian Schatell.

Fraidy Cats (0-590-46438-8)
Text copyright © 1993 by Stephen Krensky.
Illustrations copyright © 1993 by Betsy Lewin.

ISBN: 0-439-76317-7

12 11 10 9 8 7 6 5 4 3 2 1   5 6 7 8 9 10/0
Printed in the U.S.A. 56 • This compilation edition first printing, June 2005

More Spaghetti, I Say!

More Spaghetti, I Say!

by **Rita Golden Gelman**
Illustrated by **Mort Gerberg**

"Play with me, Minnie.
Play with me, please.

We can stand on our heads.
We can hang by our knees."

"Oh, no.
I can't play.
I can't play with you, Freddy.

Not now.
Can't you see?
I am eating spaghetti."

"Now you can do it.
Now you can play.

We can jump on the bed
for the rest of the day."

"No. I can **not**.
I can **not** jump and play.
Can't you see?
I need more.

More spaghetti, I say!

I love it.
I love it.
I love it.
I do.

I love it so much!"

"More than me?"

"More than you.

I love it on pancakes
with ice cream and ham.
With pickles and cookies,
bananas and jam.

I love it with mustard
and marshmallow stuff.
I eat it all day.
I just can't get enough.

I eat it on trucks,
and I eat it in trees."

"You eat it too much.
Won't you play with me,
PLEASE?"

"I can run in spaghetti.

And ride in spaghetti.

I can jump.
I can slide.
I can hide
in spaghetti.

I can skate on spaghetti,
and ski on spaghetti.

And look at this picture.
That's me on spaghetti."

"Spaghetti. Spaghetti.
That's all you can say.
I am going to throw
your spaghetti away.

I am going to throw it
all over the bed,
in the air,
on your chair,
on the floor,
ON YOUR HEAD!

Oh, Minnie,
that look on your face!
You look bad.
You look big.
You look green.
You look sick.
You look sad."

"You are right.
I am green.
I feel sick.
Yes, I do.
I think I will rest.
I will sit here with you."

"Let me take this away now.
I think that I should.

And then we can play.

Mmmmmmmm!
Spaghetti is good.

I love it.
I love it.
I love it.
I do.
I need more spaghetti.
I can't play with you."

"But **now** I can play.
I can play with you, Freddy."

"Not now.
Can't you see?

I am eating spaghetti."

The Day the Dog Said, "Cock·a· Doodle·Doo!"

The Day the Dog Said,
"Cock·a·
Doodle·Doo!"

by **David McPhail**

One sunny day,
the animals were talking.

"It's hot,"
said the duck.
"Quack!"

"Very,"
said the goose.
"Honk!"

"Moo!
Maybe it will rain,"
said the cow.

"I hope so," said the pig,
whose mud puddle was drying up.
"Oink!"

"Rain brings out the best worms,"
said the rooster.
"Cock-a-doodle-doo!"

The dog barked at the rooster.
"Stop that!
I'm trying to sleep! Woof!"

"I can't help it," said the rooster.
"I'm a rooster, and roosters say
cock-a-doodle-doo!"

Just then,
a strong wind blew
through the barnyard.
It stirred up a cloud of dust
and sent the animals
tumbling through the air.

Then it stopped.

"Is everyone all right?"
asked the duck.
"Moo!"

"I'm okay,"
said the goose.
"Oink!"

"Me, too," said the cow. "Quack!"

"Same here,"
said the pig.
"Honk!"

"I lost a few tail feathers," said the rooster. "Woof!"

Said the dog to the rooster, "I like that sound. Cock-a-doodle-doo!"

"And I like *your* sound," the rooster told the dog.

"Well, I think that the duck sounds *lovely*," said the cow.

"The goose sounds even better," said the pig.

"The cow sounds best of all!" said the duck.

"The pig is best!" said the goose.

The animals were so busy arguing
that they didn't notice
the sky grow dark.

Then, as before, a strong wind
blew through the barnyard,
stirred up a cloud of dust,
and sent the animals flying.

When the wind stopped,
a gentle rain began to fall.

No one said a word.

Then the duck spoke.
"I guess I'll go for a swim,"
he said. "Quack!"

"Wait for me," said the goose.
"Honk!"

"Moo," said the cow.
"I'm moving to the pasture
to eat some grass."

The pig jumped into a new mud puddle with a happy "Oink!"

"As for me," said the rooster,
"I've been invited to a party
at the henhouse. See you later.
Cock-a-doodle-doo!"

"Woof!" said the dog.
"It's time for a nap."

Then the barnyard was quiet—
except for the patter of raindrops,
the chatter of hens...

and the sound of a snoring dog.

Two Crazy Pigs

by **Karen Berman Nagel**

Illustrated by **Brian Schatell**

We are two crazy pigs.
We lived on the
Fenster farm.

We tickled the hens while
they were laying eggs.

"Stop that, you crazy pigs,"
yelled Mr. Fenster.

We tied the cows' tails together while they were giving milk.

"Stop that, you crazy pigs,"
yelled Mrs. Fenster.

Instead of rolling in the mud, we threw it at each other.

OOPS!

"Pack your bags and leave!"
yelled Mr. and Mrs. Fenster.

All the animals cried, "We'll miss you, crazy pigs!"

We went down the road to
Mr. and Mrs. Henhawk's farm.
"Do you have room here for
two crazy pigs?" we asked.

Mr. Henhawk made us a new
pigpen.

He laughed when we dipped
the sheep's tail in ink.

Mrs. Henhawk let us make
mud pies in her stove.

One day the Fensters' cow,
Shirley, came to visit.

"Will you come back to the
farm?" Shirley asked.

"The hens are not laying eggs.

The cows have stopped
giving milk."

"No," we said. "Mr. and
Mrs. Henhawk love us for
who we are — crazy pigs."

We pulled Shirley's tail and
said good-bye. Then she went
back to the Fenster farm.

One week later, all of the Fensters' animals came to the Henhawk farm.

Shirley spoke.
"The Fensters have moved to
the city. Do you have room
for us here?"

Mr. and Mrs. Henhawk asked all the animals to live on their farm.

We were very happy to have our friends back.

We rubbed everybody's faces in mud.

We jumped on the Henhawks' feather bed for two hours.

We were so happy! "Let's visit the Fensters in the city for old time's sake," we said.

"Are you kidding?" asked
Shirley.
"Are you sure?" asked
Mr. Henhawk.

"No," we said, "we're crazy!"

FRAIDY CATS

For my sisters and all the 'S' cats
—S.K.

To Dundee and Bones

—B.L.

FRAIDY CATS

by **Stephen Krensky**
Illustrated by **Betsy Lewin**

One dark night
when the wind blew hard,
the Fraidy Cats got ready for bed.
Scamper checked in the closet.
Nothing was there.
Sorry checked under the beds.
Nothing there, either.

They checked behind the curtains
and the door.
All was well.
They crawled into their beds
and fixed the covers.
"Good night," said Scamper.
"Pleasant dreams," said Sorry.
Then they heard a noise.

TAP, TAP, TAP!
"I hear a dog," said Sorry.
"A big hairy dog."
"Is it friendly?" Scamper asked.

"No," said Sorry.
"It likes to chase cats."
She jumped up
and shut the door.

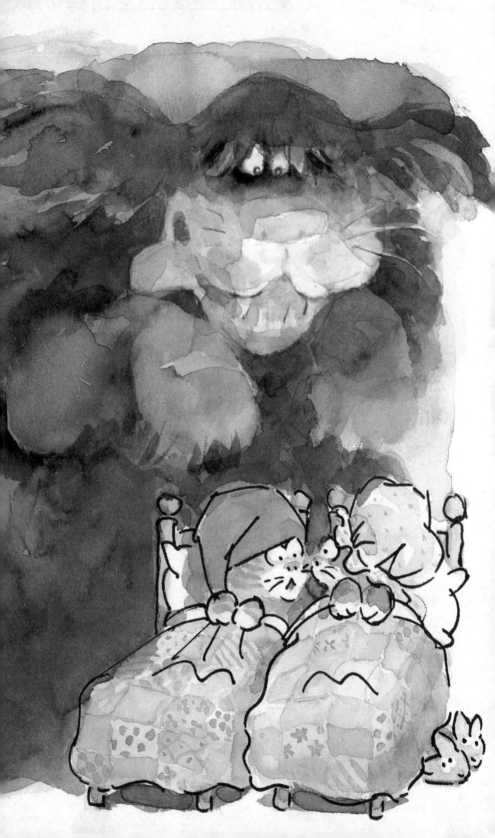

HISSSSS!
"I hear a snake," said Scamper.
"It scared the dog away."
"Is it a cute little garden snake?"
Sorry asked.

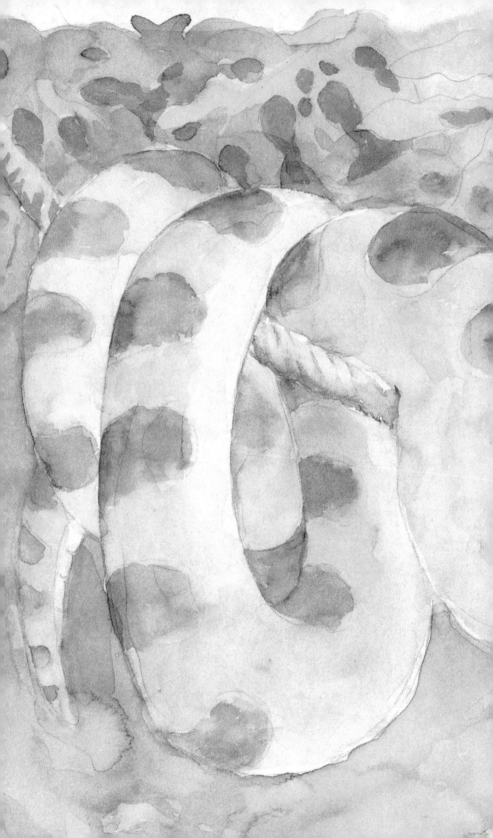

"No," said Scamper,
"It's a long giant snake
— and it hasn't eaten in a week."
He got up
and pushed a blanket
in the crack under the door.

SCREECH!
"I hear an eagle," said Sorry.
"It scared the snake away."
"Is it a gentle baby eagle?"
asked Scamper.

Sorry shook her head.
"It's a fierce mountain eagle,
swooping down from the clouds
to carry something back
to its rocky nest."
She ran to the window
and shut it.

WOOO! WOOO!
"I hear a wolf," said Scamper.
"It scared the eagle away."
"Is this a wolf that only likes to eat
three little pigs?" asked Sorry.

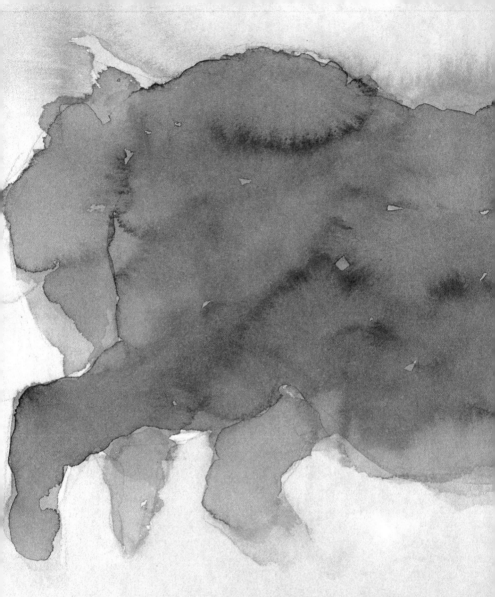

"Oh, no," said Scamper.
"This is a wolf
with many sharp teeth.
It will eat almost anything it sees."
He ran to the window
and shut the curtains.

ROOOORRR!
"I hear an elephant," said Sorry.
"It scared the wolf away."

"Is this a tame elephant
that ran away from the circus?"
Scamper asked.

"No," said Sorry.
"This is a wild elephant
with legs like tree trunks.
It crushes things that get in its way."
Scamper and Sorry
looked at each other
and dove under their beds.

BOOM! BOOM!
"I hear a dinosaur," said Scamper.
"It scared the elephant away."
"Is this a small dinosaur
the size of a lizard?" Sorry asked.
Scamper bit his lip.
"It is as big as a house," he said.

"And there's nothing left to close
or lock or hide under.
We can't stop it."
Sorry poked her head out.
"Wait a minute," she said.
"What kind of dinosaur is it?"
Scamper wasn't sure.

BOOM! BOOM! BOOM!
The room shook.
The windows rattled.
"It must be an ultrasaurus," said Sorry.
"The biggest, heaviest dinosaur
that ever lived.
We're doomed."

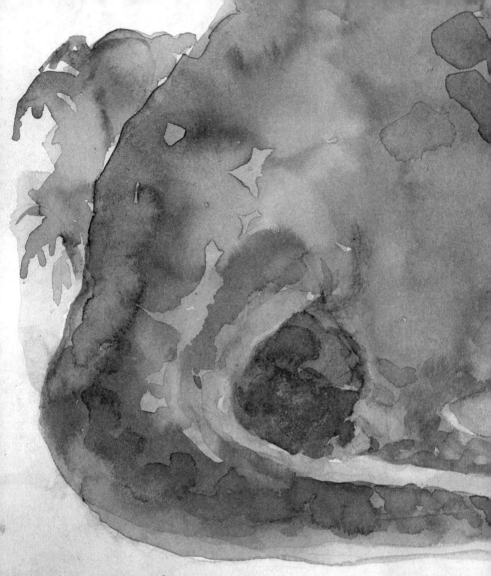

Scamper frowned.
"Wait a minute. I've read about
ultrasaurs. They only ate plants."
"Are you sure?"
"Positive."
"No cats?"
Scamper shook his head.

Sorry smiled.
"Then the ultrasaurus
will stay in the garden."
"And, it will scare away anything
else that comes by," said Scamper.
"We're safe at last."

The night was still dark.
The wind still blew hard.
The Fraidy Cats didn't care.
They got back into bed
and fixed the covers.
"Good night!" they said together,
and then fell fast asleep.